2016

Me and My Friends

My name is: _____

I live at: _____

_____

My telephone number: _____

My birthday: _____

My hobbies: _____

My greatest wish: _____

My photo

My name is: _____

I live at: _____

My photo

My telephone number: _____

My birthday: _____

In my spare time I like to: _____

My favorite animal is: _____

My favorite book: _____

My favorite singer: _____

 My favorite movie: _____

My greatest wish: _____

My wish for you: _____

At my school I'm in _____ grade.

My teacher's name is: _____

My favorite subject is: _____

My least favorite subject is: _____

My favorite holiday is: _____

My favorite food is: _____

In the future I'd like to become: _____

My photo

My name is: _____

I live at: _____

_____

My telephone number: _____

My birthday: _____

In my spare time I like to: _____

My favorite animal is: _____

My favorite book: _____

My favorite singer: _____

My favorite movie: _____

My greatest wish: _____

_____

My wish for you: _____

_____

At my school I'm in _____ grade.

My teacher's name is: _____

My favorite subject is: _____

My least favorite subject is: _____

My favorite holiday is: _____

My favorite food is: _____

In the future I'd like to become: _____

My photo

My name is:

I live at:

My telephone number:

My birthday:

In my spare time I like to:

My favorite animal is:

My favorite book:

My favorite singer:

My favorite movie:

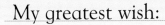

My greatest wish:

My wish for you:

At my school I'm in _____ grade.

My teacher's name is:

My favorite subject is:

My least favorite subject is:

My favorite holiday is:

My favorite food is:

In the future I'd like to become:

My name is: _____

I live at: _____

_____

My telephone number: _____

My birthday: _____

My photo

In my spare time I like to: _____

My favorite animal is: _____

My favorite book: _____

My favorite singer: _____

My favorite movie: _____

My greatest wish:

My wish for you:

At my school I'm in _____ grade.

My teacher's name is:

My favorite subject is:

My least favorite subject is:

My favorite holiday is:

My favorite food is:

In the future I'd like to become:

My name is: _____

I live at: _____

_____

My telephone number: _____

My birthday: _____

My photo

In my spare time I like to: _____

My favorite animal is: _____

My favorite book: _____

My favorite singer: _____

My favorite movie: _____

My greatest wish:

My wish for you:

At my school I'm in _____ grade.

My teacher's name is:

My favorite subject is:

My least favorite subject is:

My favorite holiday is:

My favorite food is:

In the future I'd like to become:

My photo

My name is:

I live at:

My telephone number:

My birthday:

In my spare time I like to:

My favorite animal is:

My favorite book:

My favorite singer:

My favorite movie:

My greatest wish:

My wish for you:

At my school I'm in _____ grade.

My teacher's name is:

My favorite subject is:

My least favorite subject is:

My favorite holiday is:

My favorite food is:

In the future I'd like to become:

My photo

My name is: _____

I live at: _____

_____

My telephone number: _____

My birthday: _____

In my spare time I like to: _____

My favorite animal is: _____

My favorite book: _____

My favorite singer: _____

My favorite movie: _____

My greatest wish:

My wish for you:

At my school I'm in   grade.

My teacher's name is:

My favorite subject is:

My least favorite subject is:

My favorite holiday is:

My favorite food is:

In the future I'd like to become:

My photo

My name is:

I live at:

My telephone number:

My birthday:

In my spare time I like to:

My favorite animal is:

My favorite book:

My favorite singer:

My favorite movie:

My greatest wish:

My wish for you:

At my school I'm in _____ grade.

My teacher's name is:

My favorite subject is:

My least favorite subject is:

My favorite holiday is:

My favorite food is:

In the future I'd like to become:

My name is: _____

I live at: _____

_____

My telephone number: _____

My birthday: _____

My photo

In my spare time I like to: _____

My favorite animal is: _____

My favorite book: _____

My favorite singer: _____

 My favorite movie: _____

My greatest wish: _____

My wish for you: _____

At my school I'm in _____ grade.

My teacher's name is: _____

My favorite subject is: _____

My least favorite subject is: _____

My favorite holiday is: _____

My favorite food is: _____

In the future I'd like to become: _____

My name is:

I live at:

My photo

My telephone number:

My birthday:

In my spare time I like to:

My favorite animal is:

My favorite book:

My favorite singer:

My favorite movie:

My greatest wish: _____

_____

My wish for you: _____

_____

At my school I'm in _____ grade.

My teacher's name is: _____

My favorite subject is: _____

My least favorite subject is: _____

My favorite holiday is: _____

My favorite food is: _____

In the future I'd like to become: _____

My photo

My name is:

I live at:

My telephone number:

My birthday:

In my spare time I like to:

My favorite animal is:

My favorite book:

My favorite singer:

My favorite movie:

My greatest wish: _____

My wish for you: _____

At my school I'm in _____ grade.

My teacher's name is: _____

My favorite subject is: _____

My least favorite subject is: _____

My favorite holiday is: _____

My favorite food is: _____

In the future I'd like to become: _____

My photo

My name is: _____

I live at: _____

_____

My telephone number: _____

My birthday: _____

In my spare time I like to: _____

My favorite animal is: _____

My favorite book: _____

My favorite singer: _____

My favorite movie: _____

My greatest wish:

My wish for you:

At my school I'm in _____ grade.

My teacher's name is:

My favorite subject is:

My least favorite subject is:

My favorite holiday is:

My favorite food is:

In the future I'd like to become:

My name is:

I live at:

My photo

My telephone number:

My birthday:

In my spare time I like to:

My favorite animal is:

My favorite book:

My favorite singer:

My favorite movie:

My greatest wish: _____

_____

My wish for you: _____

_____

At my school I'm in _____ grade.

My teacher's name is: _____

My favorite subject is: _____

My least favorite subject is: _____

My favorite holiday is: _____

My favorite food is: _____

In the future I'd like to become: _____

My name is: _____

I live at: _____

My photo

My telephone number: _____

My birthday: _____

In my spare time I like to: _____

My favorite animal is: _____

My favorite book: _____

My favorite singer: _____

My favorite movie: _____

My greatest wish: _____

_____

My wish for you: _____

_____

At my school I'm in _____ grade.

My teacher's name is: _____

My favorite subject is: _____

My least favorite subject is: _____

My favorite holiday is: _____

My favorite food is: _____

In the future I'd like to become: _____

My name is: _____

I live at: _____
_____

My telephone number: _____

My birthday: _____

In my spare time I like to: _____

My favorite animal is: _____

My favorite book: _____

My favorite singer: _____

My favorite movie: _____

My photo

My greatest wish: _____

My wish for you: _____

At my school I'm in _____ grade.

My teacher's name is: _____

My favorite subject is: _____

My least favorite subject is: _____

My favorite holiday is: _____

My favorite food is: _____

In the future I'd like to become: ____

My name is: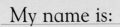

I live at:

My photo

My telephone number:

My birthday:

In my spare time I like to:

My favorite animal is:

My favorite book:

My favorite singer:

My favorite movie:

My greatest wish:

My wish for you:

At my school I'm in   grade.

My teacher's name is:

My favorite subject is:

My least favorite subject is:

My favorite holiday is:

My favorite food is:

In the future I'd like to become:

My name is: _____

I live at: _____

_____

My telephone number: _____

My birthday: _____

In my spare time I like to: _____

My favorite animal is: _____

My favorite book: _____

My favorite singer: _____

 My favorite movie: _____

My photo

My greatest wish: _____

_____

My wish for you: _____

_____

At my school I'm in _____ grade.

My teacher's name is: _____

My favorite subject is: _____

My least favorite subject is: _____

My favorite holiday is: _____

My favorite food is: _____

In the future I'd like to become: _____

My name is: _____

I live at: _____

My photo

_____

My telephone number: _____

My birthday: _____

In my spare time I like to: _____

My favorite animal is: _____

My favorite book: _____

My favorite singer: _____

My favorite movie: _____

My greatest wish:

My wish for you:

At my school I'm in   grade.

My teacher's name is:

My favorite subject is:

My least favorite subject is:

My favorite holiday is:

My favorite food is:

In the future I'd like to become:

My name is:

I live at:

My photo

My telephone number:

My birthday:

In my spare time I like to:

My favorite animal is:

My favorite book:

My favorite singer:

My favorite movie:

My greatest wish:

My wish for you:

At my school I'm in   grade.

My teacher's name is:

My favorite subject is:

My least favorite subject is:

My favorite holiday is:

My favorite food is:

In the future I'd like to become:

My photo

My name is:

I live at:

My telephone number:

My birthday:

In my spare time I like to:

My favorite animal is:

My favorite book:

My favorite singer:

My favorite movie:

My greatest wish:

My wish for you:

At my school I'm in _____ grade.

My teacher's name is:

My favorite subject is:

My least favorite subject is:

My favorite holiday is:

My favorite food is:

In the future I'd like to become:

My name is:

I live at:

My photo

My telephone number:

My birthday:

In my spare time I like to:

My favorite animal is:

My favorite book:

My favorite singer:

My favorite movie:

My greatest wish: _____

_____

My wish for you: _____

At my school I'm in _____ grade.

My teacher's name is: _____

My favorite subject is: _____

My least favorite subject is: _____

My favorite holiday is: _____

My favorite food is: _____

In the future I'd like to become: _____

My name is: _____

I live at: _____

_____

My photo

My telephone number: _____

My birthday: _____

In my spare time I like to: _____

My favorite animal is: _____

My favorite book: _____

My favorite singer: _____

My favorite movie: _____

My greatest wish:

My wish for you:

At my school I'm in _____ grade.

My teacher's name is:

My favorite subject is:

My least favorite subject is:

My favorite holiday is:

My favorite food is:

In the future I'd like to become:

My name is: _____

I live at: _____

_____

My telephone number: _____

My birthday: _____

In my spare time I like to: _____

My favorite animal is: _____

My favorite book: _____

My favorite singer: _____

My favorite movie: _____

My photo

My greatest wish: _____

My wish for you: _____

At my school I'm in _____ grade.

My teacher's name is: _____

My favorite subject is: _____

My least favorite subject is: _____

My favorite holiday is: _____

My favorite food is: _____

In the future I'd like to become: _____

My name is:

I live at:

My telephone number:

My birthday:

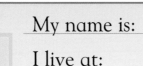

My photo

In my spare time I like to:

My favorite animal is:

My favorite book:

My favorite singer:

My favorite movie:

My greatest wish:

My wish for you:

At my school I'm in _____ grade.

My teacher's name is:

My favorite subject is:

My least favorite subject is:

My favorite holiday is:

My favorite food is:

In the future I'd like to become:

My name is: _____

I live at: _____

_____

My photo

My telephone number: _____

My birthday: _____

In my spare time I like to: _____

My favorite animal is: _____

My favorite book: _____

My favorite singer: _____

My favorite movie: _____

My greatest wish: _____

_____

My wish for you: _____

_____

At my school I'm in _____ grade.

My teacher's name is: _____

My favorite subject is: _____

My least favorite subject is: _____

My favorite holiday is: _____

My favorite food is: _____

In the future I'd like to become: _____

My name is: _____

I live at: _____

_____

My telephone number: _____

My birthday: _____

In my spare time I like to: _____

My favorite animal is: _____

My favorite book: _____

My favorite singer: _____

My favorite movie: _____

My photo

My greatest wish: _____

_____

My wish for you: _____

_____

At my school I'm in _____ grade.

My teacher's name is: _____

My favorite subject is: _____

My least favorite subject is: _____

My favorite holiday is: _____

My favorite food is: _____

In the future I'd like to become: _____

My name is:

I live at:

My photo

My telephone number:

My birthday:

In my spare time I like to:

My favorite animal is:

My favorite book:

My favorite singer:

My favorite movie:

My greatest wish:

My wish for you:

At my school I'm in _____ grade.

My teacher's name is:

My favorite subject is:

My least favorite subject is:

My favorite holiday is:

My favorite food is:

In the future I'd like to become:

My photo

My name is:

I live at:

My telephone number:

My birthday:

In my spare time I like to:

My favorite animal is:

My favorite book:

My favorite singer:

My favorite movie:

My greatest wish:

My wish for you:

At my school I'm in _____ grade.

My teacher's name is:

My favorite subject is:

My least favorite subject is:

My favorite holiday is:

My favorite food is:

In the future I'd like to become: